The Man of Letters as a Man of Business

William Dean Howells

Contents

THE MAN OF LETTERS AS A MAN OF BUSINESS

BY

William Dean Howells

"THE MAN OF LETTERS AS A MAN OF BUSINESS"
by
William Dean Howells

I think that every man ought to work for his living, without exception, and that when he has once avouched his willingness to work, society should provide him with work and warrant him a living. I do not think any man ought to live by an art. A man's art should be his privilege, when he has proven his fitness to exercise it, and has otherwise earned his daily bread; and its results should be free to all. There is an instinctive sense of this, even in the midst of the grotesque confusion of our economic being; people feel that there is something profane, something impious, in taking money for a picture, or a poem, or a statue. Most of all, the artist himself feels this. He puts on a bold front with the world, to be sure, and brazens it out as Business; but he knows very well that there is something false and vulgar in it; and that the work which cannot be truly priced in money cannot be truly paid in money. He can, of course, say that the priest takes money for reading the marriage service, for christening the new-born babe, and for saying the last office for the dead; that the physician sells healing; that justice itself is paid for; and that he is merely a party to the thing that is and must be. He can say that, as the thing is, unless he sells his art he cannot live, that society will leave him to starve if he does not hit its fancy in a picture, or a poem, or a statue; and all this is bitterly true. He is, and he must be, only too glad if there is a market for his wares. Without a market for his wares he must perish, or turn to making something that will sell better than pictures, or poems, or statues. All the same, the sin and the shame remain, and the averted eye sees them still, with its inward vision. Many will make believe otherwise, but I would rather not make believe otherwise; and in trying to write of Literature as Business I am tempted to begin by saying that Business is the op-probrium of Literature.

II.

Literature is at once the most intimate and the most articulate of the arts. It cannot impart its effect through the senses or the nerves as the other arts can; it is beautiful only through the intelligence; it is the mind speaking to the mind; until it has been put into absolute terms, of an invariable significance, it does not exist at all. It cannot awaken this emotion in one, and that in another; if it fails to express precisely the meaning of the author, if it does not say HIM, it says nothing, and is nothing. So that when a poet has put his heart, much or little, into a poem, and sold it to a magazine, the scandal is greater than when a painter has sold a picture to a patron, or a sculptor has modelled a statue to order. These are artists less articulate and less intimate than the poet; they are more exterior to their work; they are less personally in it; they part with less of themselves in the dicker. It does not change the nature of the case to say that Tennyson and Longfellow and Emerson sold the poems in which they couched the most mystical messages their genius was charged to bear mankind. They submitted to the conditions which none can escape; but that does not justify the conditions, which are none the less the conditions of hucksters because they are imposed upon poets. If it will serve to make my meaning a little clearer we will suppose that a poet has been crossed in love, or has suffered some real sorrow, like the loss of a wife or child. He pours out his broken heart in verse that shall bring tears of sacred sympathy from his readers, and an editor pays him a hundred dollars for the right of bringing his verse to their notice. It is perfectly true that the poem was not written for these dollars, but it is perfectly true that it was sold for them. The poet must use his emotions to pay his provision bills; he has no other means; society does not propose to pay his bills for him. Yet, and at the end of the ends, the unsophisticated witness finds the transaction ridiculous, finds it repulsive, finds it shabby. Somehow he knows that if our huckstering civilization did not at every moment violate the eternal fitness of things, the poet's song would have been given to the world, and the poet would have been cared for by the whole human brotherhood, as any man should be who does the duty that every man owes it.

The instinctive sense of the dishonor which money-purchase does to art is so strong that sometimes a man of letters who can pay his way otherwise refuses pay for his work, as Lord Byron did, for a while, from a noble pride, and as Count Tolstoy has tried to do, from a noble conscience. But Byron's publisher profited by a generosity which did not reach his readers; and the Countess Tolstoy collects the copyright which her husband foregoes; so that these two eminent instances of protest against business in literature may be said not to have shaken its money basis. I know of no others; but there may be many that I am culpably ignorant of. Still, I doubt if there are enough to affect the fact that Literature is Business as well as Art, and almost as soon. At present business is the only human solidarity; we are all bound together with that chain, whatever interests and tastes and principles separate us, and I feel quite sure that in writing of the Man of Letters as a Man of Business, I shall attract far more readers than I should in writing of him as an Artist. Besides, as an artist he has been done a great deal already; and a commercial state like ours has really more concern in him as a business man. Perhaps it may sometimes be different; I do not believe it will till the conditions are different, and that is a long way off.

III.

In the meantime I confidently appeal to the reader's imagination with the fact that there are several men of letters among us who are such good men of business that they can command a hundred dollars a thousand words for all they write; and at least one woman of letters who gets a hundred and fifty dollars a thousand words. It is easy to write a thousand words a day, and supposing one of these authors to work steadily, it can be seen that his net earnings during the year would come to some such sum as the President of the United States gets for doing far less work of a much more perishable sort. If the man of letters were wholly a business man this is what would happen; he would make his forty or fifty thousand dollars a year, and be able to consort with bank presidents, and railroad officials, and rich tradesmen, and other flowers of our plutocracy on equal terms. But, unfortunately, from a business point of view, he is also an artist, and the very qualities that enable him to delight the public disable him from delighting it uninterruptedly. "No rose blooms right along," as the English boys at Oxford made an American collegian say in a theme which they imagined for him in his national parlance; and the man of letters, as an artist, is apt to have times and seasons when he cannot blossom. Very often it shall happen that his mind will lie fallow between novels or stories for weeks and months at a stretch; when the suggestions of the friendly editor shall fail to fruit in the essays or articles desired; when the muse shall altogether withhold herself, or shall respond only in a feeble dribble of verse which he might sell indeed, but which it would not be good business for him to put on the market. But supposing him to be a very diligent and continuous worker, and so happy as to have fallen on a theme that delights him and bears him along, he may please himself so ill with the result of his labors that he can do nothing less in artistic conscience than destroy a day's work, a week's work, a month's work. I know one man of letters who wrote to-day, and tore up tomorrow for nearly a whole summer. But even if part of the mistaken work may be saved, because it is good work out of place, and not intrinsically bad, the task of reconstruction wants almost as much time as the production; and then, when all seems done, comes the anxious and endless process of revision. These drawbacks reduce the earning capacity of what I may call the high-cost man of letters in such measure that an author whose name is known everywhere, and whose reputation is commensurate with the boundaries of his country, if it does not transcend them, shall have the income, say, of a rising young physician, known to a few people in a subordinate city.

In view of this fact, so humiliating to an author in the presence of a nation of business men like ours, I do not know that I can establish the man of letters in the popular esteem as very much of a business man after all. He must still have a low rank among practical people; and he will be regarded by the great mass of Americans as perhaps a little off, a little funny, a little soft!

Perhaps not; and yet I would rather not have a consensus of public opinion on the question; I think I am more comfortable without it.

IV.

There is this to be said in defence of men of letters on the business side, that literature is still an infant industry with us, and so far from having been protected by our laws it was exposed for ninety years after the foundation of the republic to the vicious competition of stolen goods. It is true that we now have the international copyright law at last, and we can at least begin to forget our shame; but literary property has only forty-two years of life under our unjust statutes, and if it is attacked by robbers the law does not seek out the aggressors and punish them, as it would seek out and punish the trespassers upon any other kind of property; but it leaves the aggrieved owner to bring suit against them, and recover damages, if he can. This may be right enough in itself; but I think, then, that all property should be defended by civil suit, and should become public after forty-two years of private tenure. The Constitution guarantees us all equality before the law, but the law-makers seem to have forgotten this in the case of our infant literary industry. So long as this remains the case, we cannot expect the best business talent to go into literature, and the man of letters must keep his present low grade among business men.

As I have hinted, it is but a little while that he has had any standing at all. I may say that it is only since the was that literature has become a business with us. Before that time we had authors, and very good ones; it is astonishing how good they were; but I do not remember any of them who lived by literature except Edgar A. Poe, perhaps; and we all know how he lived; it was largely upon loans. They were either men of fortune, or they were editors, or professors, with salaries or incomes apart from the small gains of their pens; or they were helped out with public offices; one need not go over their names, or classify them. Some of them must have made money by their books, but I question whether any one could have lived, even very simply, upon the money his books brought him. No one could do that now, unless he wrote a book that we could not recognize as a work of literature. But many authors live now, and live prettily enough, by the sale of the serial publication of their writings to the magazines. They do not live so nicely as successful tradespeople, of course, or as men in the other professions when they begin to make themselves names; the high state of brokers, bankers, railroad operators, and the like is, in the nature of the case, beyond their fondest dreams of pecuniary affluence and social splendor. Perhaps they do not want the chief seats in the synagogue; it is certain they do not get them. Still, they do very fairly well, as things go; and several have incomes that would seem riches to the great mass of worthy Americans who work with their hands for a living--when they can get the work. Their incomes are mainly from serial publication in the different magazines; and the prosperity of the magazines has given a whole class existence which, as a class, was wholly unknown among us before the war. It is not only the famous or fully recognized authors who live in this way, but the much larger number of clever people who are as yet known chiefly to the editors, and who may never make themselves a public, but who do well a kind of acceptable work. These are the sort who do not get reprinted from the periodicals; but the better recognized authors do get reprinted, and then their serial work in its completed form appeals to the readers who say they do not read serials. The multitude of these is not great, and if an author rested his hopes upon their favor he would be a much more embittered man than he now generally is. But he understands perfectly well that his reward is in the serial and not in the book; the return from that he may count as so much money found in the road--a few hundreds, a very few thousands, at the most.

V.

I doubt, indeed, whether the earnings of literary men are absolutely as great as they were earlier in the century, in any of the English-speaking countries; relatively they are nothing like as great. Scott had forty thousand dollars for "Woodstock," which was not a very large novel, and was by no means one of his best; and forty thousand dollars had at least the purchasing powers of sixty thousand then. Moore had three thousand guineas for "Lalla Rookh," but what publisher would be rash enough to pay twenty-five thousand dollars for the masterpiece of a minor poet now? The book, except in very rare instances, makes nothing like the return to the author that the magazine makes, and there are but two or three authors who find their account in that form of publication. Those who do, those who sell the most widely in book form, are often not at all desired by editors; with difficulty they get a serial accepted by any principal magazine. On the other hand, there are authors whose books, compared with those of the popular favorites, do not sell, and yet they are eagerly sought for by editors; they are paid the highest prices, and nothing that they offer is refused. These are literary artists; and it ought to be plain from what I am saying that in belles-lettres, at least, most of the best literature now first sees the light in the magazines, and most of the second best appears first in book form. The old-fashioned people who flatter themselves upon their distinction in not reading magazine fiction, or magazine poetry, make a great mistake, and simply class themselves with the public whose taste is so crude that they cannot enjoy the best. Of course this is true mainly, if not merely, of belles-lettres; history, science, politics, metaphysics, in spite of the many excellent articles and papers in these sorts upon what used to be called various emergent occasions, are still to be found at their best in books. The most monumental example of literature, at once light and good, which has first reached the public in book form is in the different publications of Mark Twain; but Mr. Clemens has of late turned to the magazines too, and now takes their mint mark before he passes into general circulation. All this may change again, but at present the magazines--we have no longer any reviews--form the most direct approach to that part of our reading public which likes the highest things in literary art. Their readers, if we may judge from the quality of the literature they get, are more refined than the book readers in our community; and their taste has no doubt been cultivated by that of the disciplined and experienced editors. So far as I have known these they are men of aesthetic conscience, and of generous sympathy. They have their preferences in the different kinds, and they have their theory of what kind will be most acceptable to their readers; but they exercise their selective function with the wish to give them the best things they can. I do not know one of them--and it has been my good fortune to know them nearly all--who would print a wholly inferior thing for the sake of an inferior class of readers, though they may sometimes decline a good thing because for one reason or another they believe it would not be liked. Still, even this does not often happen; they would rather chance the good thing they doubted of than underrate their readers' judgment.

New writers often suppose themselves rejected because they are unknown; but the unknown man of force and quality is of all others the man whom the editor welcomes to his page. He knows that there is always a danger that the reigning favorite may fail to please; that at any rate, in the order of things, he is passing away, and that if the magazine is not to pass away with the men who have made it, there must be a constant infusion of fresh life. Few editors are such fools and knaves as to let their personal feeling disable their judgment; and the young writer who gets his manuscript back may be sure that it is not because the editor dislikes him, for some reason or no reason. Above all, he can trust me that his contribution has not been passed unread, or has failed of the examination it merits. Editors are not men of infallible judgment, but they do use their judgment, and it is usually good.

The young author who wins recognition in a first-class magazine has achieved a double success, first, with the editor, and then with the best reading public. Many factitious and fallacious literary reputations have been made through books, but very few have been made through the magazines, which are not only the best means of living, but of outliving, with the author; they are both bread and fame to him. If I insist a little upon the high office which this modern form of publication fulfils in the literary world, it is because I am impatient of the antiquated and ignorant prejudice which classes the magazines as ephemeral. They are ephemeral in form, but in substance they are not ephemeral, and what is best in them awaits its resurrection in the book, which, as the first form, is so often a lasting death. An interesting proof of the value of the magazine to literature is the fact that a good novel will have wider acceptance as a book from having been a magazine serial.

I am not sure that the decay of the book is not owing somewhat to the decay of reviewing. This does not now seem to me so thorough, or even so general as it was some years ago, and I think the book oftener comes to the buyer without the warrant of a critical estimate than it once did. That is never the case with material printed in a magazine of high class. A well-trained critic, who is bound by the strongest ties of honor and interest not to betray either his employer or his public, has judged it, and his practical approval is a warrant of quality.

VI.

Under the regime of the great literary periodicals the prosperity of literary men would be much greater than it actually is, if the magazines were altogether literary. But they are not, and this is one reason why literature is still the hungriest of the professions. Two-thirds of the magazines are made up of material which, however excellent, is without literary quality. Very probably this is because even the highest class of readers, who are the magazine readers, have small love of pure literature, which seems to have been growing less and less in all classes. I say seems, because there are really no means of ascertaining the fact, and it may be that the editors are mistaken in making their periodicals two-thirds popular science, politics, economics, and the timely topics which I will call contemporaries; I have sometimes thought they were. But however that may be, their efforts in this direction have narrowed the field of literary industry, and darkened the hope of literary prosperity kindled by the unexampled prosperity of their periodicals. They pay very well indeed for literature; they pay from five or six dollars a thousand words for the work of the unknown writer, to a hundred and fifty dollars a thousand words for that of the most famous, or the most popular, if there is a difference between fame and popularity; but they do not, altogether, want enough literature to justify the best business talent in devoting itself to belles-lettres, to fiction, or poetry, or humorous sketches of travel, or light essays; business talent can do far better in drygoods, groceries, drugs, stocks, real estate, railroads, and the like. I do not think there is any danger of a ruinous competition from it in the field which, though narrow, seems so rich to us poor fellows, whose business talent is small, at the best.

The most of the material contributed to the magazines is the subject of agreement between the editor and the author; it is either suggested by the author, or is the fruit of some suggestion from the editor; in any case the price is stipulated beforehand, and it is no longer the custom for a well-known contributor to leave the payment to the justice or the generosity of the publisher; that was never a fair thing to either, nor ever a wise thing. Usually, the price is so much a thousand words, a truly odious method of computing literary value, and one well calculated to make the author feel keenly the hatefulness of selling his art at all. It is as if a painter sold his picture at so much a square inch, or a sculptor bargained away a group of statuary by the pound. But it is a custom that you cannot always successfully quarrel with, and most writers gladly consent to it, if only the price a thousand words is large enough. The sale to the editor means the sale of the serial rights only, but if the publisher of the magazine is also a publisher of books, the republication of the material is supposed to be his right, unless there is an understanding to the contrary; the terms for this are another affair. Formerly something more could be got for the author by the simultaneous appearance of his work in an English magazine, but now the great American magazines, which pay far higher prices than any others in the world, have a circulation in England so much exceeding that of any English periodical, that the simultaneous publication can no longer be arranged for from this side, though I believe it is still done here from the other side.

VII.

I think this is the case of authorship as it now stands with regard to the magazines. I am not sure that the case is in every way improved for young authors. The magazines all maintain a staff for the careful examination of manuscripts, but as most of the material they print has been engaged, the number of volunteer contributions that they can use is very small; one of the greatest of them, I know, does not use fifty in the course of a year. The new writer, then, must be very good to be accepted, and when accepted he may wait long before he is printed. The pressure is so great in these avenues to the public favor that one, two, three years, are no uncommon periods of delay. If the writer has not the patience for this, or has a soul above cooling his heels in the courts of fame, or must do his best to earn something at once, the book is his immediate hope. How slight a hope the book is I have tried to hint already, but if a book is vulgar enough in sentiment, and crude enough in taste, and flashy enough in incident, or, better or worse still, if it is a bit hot in the mouth, and promises impropriety if not indecency, there is a very fair chance of its success; I do not mean success with a self-respecting publisher, but with the public, which does not personally put its name to it, and is not openly smirched by it. I will not talk of that kind of book, however, but of the book which the young author has written out of an unspoiled heart and an untainted mind, such as most young men and women write; and I will suppose that it has found a publisher. It is human nature, as competition has deformed human nature, for the publisher to wish the author to take all the risks, and he possibly proposes that the author shall publish it at his own expense, and let him have a percentage of the retail price for managing it. If not that, he proposes that the author shall pay for the stereotype plates, and take fifteen per cent. of the price of the book; or if this will not go, if the author cannot, rather than will not do it (he is commonly only too glad to do anything he can), then the publisher offers him ten per cent. of the retail price after the first thousand copies have been sold. But if he fully believes in the book, he will give ten per cent. from the first copy sold, and pay all the costs of publication himself. The book is to be retailed for a dollar and a half, and the publisher is very well pleased with a new book that sells fifteen hundred copies. Whether the author has as much reason to be so is a question, but if the book does not sell more he has only himself to blame, and had better pocket in silence the two hundred and twenty-five dollars he gets for it, and bless his publisher, and try to find work somewhere at five dollars a week. The publisher has not made any more, if quite as much as the author, and until a book has sold two thousand copies the division is fair enough. After that, the heavier expenses of manufacturing have been defrayed, and the book goes on advertising itself; there is merely the cost of paper, printing, binding, and market-ing to be met, and the arrangement becomes fairer and fairer for the publisher. The author has no right to complain of this, in the case of his first book, which he is only too grateful to get accepted at all. If it succeeds, he has himself to blame for making the same arrangement for his second or third; it is his fault, or else it is his necessity, which is practically the same thing. It will be business for the publisher to take advantage of his necessity quite the same as if it were his fault; but I do not say that he will always do so; I believe he will very often not do so.

At one time there seemed a probability of the enlargement of the author's gains by subscription publication, and one very well-known American author prospered fabulously in that way. The percentage offered by the subscription houses was only about half as much as that paid by the trade, but the sales were so much greater that the author could very well afford to take it. Where the book-dealer sold ten, the book-agent sold a hundred; or at least he did so in the case of Mark Twain's books; and we all thought it reasonable he could do so with ours. Such of us as made experiment of him, however, found the facts illogical. No book of literary quality was made to go by subscription except Mr. Clemens's books, and I think these went because the subscription public never knew what good literature they were. This sort of readers, or buyers, were so used to getting something worthless for their money, that they would not spend it for artistic fiction, or indeed for any fiction all, except Mr. Clemens's, which they probably supposed bad. Some good books of travel had a measurable success through the book agents, but not at all the success that had been hoped for; and I believe now the subscription trade again publishes only compilations, or such works as owe more to the skill of the editor than the art of the writer. Mr. Clemens himself no longer offers his books to the public in that way.

It is not common, I think, in this country, to publish on the half-profits system, but it is very common in England, where, owing probably to the moisture in the air, which lends a fairy outline to every prospect, it seems to be peculiarly alluring. One of my own early books was published there on these terms, which I accepted with the insensate joy of the young author in getting any terms from a publisher. The book sold, sold every copy of the small first edition, and in due time the publisher's statement came. I did not think my half of the profits was very great, but it seemed a fair division after every imaginable cost had been charged up against my poor book, and that frail venture had been made to pay the expenses of composition, corrections, paper, printing, binding, advertising, and editorial copies. The wonder ought to have been that there was anything at all coming to me, but I was young and greedy then, and I really thought there ought to have been more. I was disappointed, but I made the best of it, of course, and took the account to the junior partner of the house which employed me, and said that I should like to draw on him for the sum due me from the London publishers. He said, Certainly; but after a glance at the account he smiled and said he supposed I knew how much the sum was? I answered, Yes; it was eleven pounds nine shillings, was not it? But I owned at the same time that I never was good at figures, and that I found English money peculiarly baffling. He laughed now, and said, It was eleven shillings and nine pence. In fact, after all those charges for composition, corrections, paper, printing, binding, advertising, and editorial copies, there was a most ingenious and wholly surprising charge of ten per cent. commission on sales, which reduced my half from pounds to shillings, and handsomely increased the publisher's half in proportion. I do not now dispute the justice of the charge. It was not the fault of the half-profits system, it was the fault of the glad young author who did not distinctly inform himself of its mysterious nature in agreeing to it, and had only to reproach himself if he was finally disappointed.

But there is always something disappointing in the accounts of publishers, which I fancy is because authors are strangely constituted, rather than because publishers are so. I will confess that I have such inordinate expectations of the sale of my books which I hope I think modestly of, that the sales reported to me never seem great enough. The copyright due me, no matter how handsome it is, appears deplorably mean, and I feel impoverished for several days after I get it. But then, I ought to add that my balance in the bank is always much less than I have supposed it to be, and my own checks, when they come back to me, have the air of having been in a conspiracy to betray me.

No, we literary men must learn, no matter how we boast ourselves in business, that the distress we feel from our publisher's accounts is simply idiopathic; and I for one wish to bear my witness to the constant good faith and uprightness of publishers.

It is supposed that because they have the affair altogether in their hands they are apt to take advantage in it; but this does not follow, and as a matter of fact they have the affair no more in their own hands than any other business man you have an open account with. There is nothing to prevent you from looking at their books, except your own innermost belief and fear that their books are correct, and that your literature has brought you so little because it has sold so little.

The author is not to blame for his superficial delusion to the contrary, especially if he has written a book that has set everyone talking, because it is of a vital interest. It may be of a vital interest, without being at all the kind of book people want to buy; it may be the kind of book that they are content to know at second hand; there are such fatal books; but hearing so much, and reading so much about it, the author cannot help hoping that it has sold much more than the publisher says. The publisher is undoubtedly honest, however, and the author had better put away the comforting question of his integrity.

The English writers seem largely to suspect their publishers (I cannot say with how much reason, for my English publisher is Scotch, and I should be glad to be so true a man as I think him); but I believe that American authors, when not flown with flattering reviews, as largely trust theirs. Of course there are rogues in every walk of life. I will not say that I ever personally met them in the flowery paths of literature, but I have heard of other people meeting them there, just as I have heard of people seeing ghosts, and I have to believe in both the rogues and the ghosts, without the witness of my own senses. I suppose, upon such grounds mainly, that there are wicked publishers, but in the case of our books that do not sell, I am afraid that it is the graceless and inappreciative public which is far more to blame than the wickedest of the publishers. It is true that publishers will drive a hard bargain when they can, or when they must; but there is nothing to hinder an author from driving a hard bargain, too, when he can, or when he must; and it is to be said of the publisher that he is always more willing to abide by the bargain when it is made than the author is; perhaps because he has the best of it. But he has not always the best of it; I have known publishers too generous to take advantage of the innocence of authors; and I fancy that if publishers had to do with any race less diffident than authors, they would have won a repute for unselfishness that they do not now enjoy. It is certain that in the long period when we flew the black flag of piracy there were many among our corsairs on the high seas of literature who paid a fair price for the stranger craft they seized; still oftener they removed the cargo, and released their capture with several weeks' provision; and although there was undoubtedly a good deal of actual throat-cutting and scuttling, still I feel sure that there was less of it than there would have been in any other line of business released to the unrestricted plunder of the neighbor. There was for a long time even a comity among these amiable buccaneers, who agreed not to interfere with each other, and so were enabled to pay over to their victims some portion of the profit from their stolen goods. Of all business men publishers are probably the most faithful and honorable, and are only surpassed in virtue when men of letters turn business men.

Publishers have their little theories, their little superstitions, and their blind faith in the great god Chance, which we all worship. These things lead them into temptation and adversity, but they seem to do fairly well as business men, even in their own behalf. They do not make above the usual ninety-five per cent. of failures, and more publishers than authors get rich. I have known several publishers who kept their carriages, but I have never known even one author to keep his carriage on the profits of his literature, unless it was in some modest country place where one could take care of one's own horse. But this is simply because the authors are so many, and the publishers are so few. If we wish to reverse their positions, we must study how to reduce the number of authors and increase the number of publishers; then prosperity will smile our way.

VIII.

Some theories or superstitions publishers and authors share together. One of these is that it is best to keep your books all in the hands of one publisher if you can, because then he can give them more attention ad sell more of them. But my own experience is that when my books were in the hands of three publishers they sold quite as well as when one had them; and a fellow author whom I approached in question of this venerable belief, laughed at it. This bold heretic held that it was best to give each new book to a new publisher, for then the fresh man put all his energies into pushing it; but if you had them all together, the publisher rested in a vain security that one book would sell another, and that the fresh venture would revive the public interest in the stale ones. I never knew this to happen, and I must class it with the superstitions of the trade. It may be so in other and more constant countries, but in our fickle republic, each last book has to fight its own way to public favor, much as if it had no sort of literary lineage. Of course this is stating it rather largely, and the truth will be found inside rather than outside of my statement; but there is at least truth enough in it to give the young author pause. While one is preparing to sell his basket of glass, he may as well ask himself whether it is better to part with all to one dealer or not; and if he kicks it over, in spurning the imaginary customer who asks the favor of taking entire stock, that will be his fault, and not the fault of the question.

However, the most important question of all with the man of letters as a man of business, is what kind of book will sell the best of itself, because, at the end of the ends, a book sells itself or does not sell at all; kissing, after long ages of reasoning and a great deal of culture, still goes by favor, and though innumerable generations of horses have been led to water, not one horse has yet been made to drink. With the best, or the worst, will in the world, no publisher can force a book into acceptance. Advertising will not avail, and reviewing is notoriously futile. If the book does not strike the popular fancy, or deal with some universal interest, which need by no means be a profound or important one, the drums and the cymbals shall be beaten in vain. The book may be one of the best and wisest books in the world, but if it has not this sort of appeal in it, the readers of it, and worse yet, the purchasers, will remain few, though fit. The secret of this, like most other secrets of a rather ridiculous world, is in the awful keeping of fate, and we can only hope to surprise it by some lucky chance. To plan a surprise of it, to aim a book at the public favor, is the most hopeless of all endeavors, as it is one of the unworthiest; and I can, neither as a man of letters nor as a man of business, counsel the young author to do it. The best that you can do is to write the book that it gives you the most pleasure to write, to put as much heart and soul as you have about you into it, and then hope as hard as you can to reach the heart and soul of the great multitude of your fellow-men. That, and that alone, is good business for a man of letters.

The failures in literature are no less mystifying than the successes, though they are upon the whole not so mortifying. I have seen a good many of these failures, and I know of one case so signal that I must speak of it, even to the discredit of the public. It is the case of a novelist whose work seems to me of the best that we have done in that sort, whose books represent our life with singular force and singular insight, and whose equipment for his art, through study, travel, and the world, is of the rarest. He has a strong, robust, manly style; his stories are well knit, and his characters are of the flesh and blood complexion which we know in our daily experience; and yet he has failed to achieve one of the first places in our literature; if I named his name here, I am afraid that it would be quite unknown to the greatest part of my readers. I have never been able to account for his want of success, except through the fact that his stories did not please women, though why they did not, I cannot guess. They did not like them for the same reason that they did not like Dr. Fell; and that reason was quite enough for them. It must be enough for him, I am afraid; but I believe that if this author had been writing in a country where men decided the fate of books, the fate of his books would have been different.

The man of letters must make up his mind that in the United States the fate of a book is in the hands of the women. It is the women with us who have the most leisure, and they read the most books. They are far better educated, for the most part, than our men, and their tastes, if not their minds, are more cultivated. Our men read the newspapers, but our women read the books; the more refined among them read the magazines. If they do not always know what is good, they do know what pleases them, and it is useless to quarrel with their decisions, for there is no appeal from them. To go from them to the men would be going from a higher to a lower court, which would be honestly surprised and bewildered, if the thing were possible. As I say, the author of light literature, and often the author of solid literature, must resign himself to obscurity unless the ladies choose to recognize him. Yet it would be impossible to forecast their favor for this kind or that. Who could prophesy it for another, who guess it for himself? We must strive blindly for it, and hope somehow that our best will also be our prettiest; but we must remember at the same time that it is not the ladies' man who is the favorite of the ladies.

There are of course a few, a very few, of our greatest authors, who have striven forward to the first place in our Valhalla without the help of the largest reading-class among us; but I should say that these were chiefly the humorists, for whom women are said nowhere to have any warm liking, and who have generally with us come up through the newspapers, and have never lost the favor of the newspaper readers. They have become literary men, as it were, without the newspapers' readers knowing it; but those who have approached literature from another direction, have won fame in it chiefly by grace of the women, who first read them, and then made their husbands and fathers read them. Perhaps, then, and as a matter of business, it would be well for a serious author, when he finds that he is not pleasing the women, and probably never will please them, to turn humorous author, and aim at the countenance of the men. Except as a humorist he certainly never will get it, for your American, when he is not making money, or trying to do it, is making a joke, or trying to do it.

IX.

I hope that I have not been hinting that the author who approaches literature through journalism is not as fine and high a literary man as the author who comes directly to it, or through some other avenue; I have not the least notion of condemning myself by any such judgment. But I think it is pretty certain that fewer and fewer authors are turning from journalism to literature, though the entente cordiale between the two professions seems as great as ever. I fancy, though I may be as mistaken in this as I am in a good many other things, that most journalists would have been literary men if they could, at the beginning, and that the kindness they almost always show to young authors is an effect of the self-pity they feel for their own thwarted wish to be authors. When an author is once warm in the saddle, and is riding his winged horse to glory, the case is different: they have then often no sentiment about him; he is no longer the image of their own young aspiration, and they would willingly see Pegasus buck under him, or have him otherwise brought to grief and shame. They are apt to gird at him for his unhallowed gains, and they would be quite right in this if they proposed any way for him to live without them; as I have allowed at the outset, the gains ARE unhallowed. Apparently it is unseemly for an author or two to be making half as much by their pens as popular ministers often receive in salary; the public is used to the pecuniary prosperity of some of the clergy, and at least sees nothing droll in it; but the paragrapher can always get a smile out of his readers at the gross disparity between the ten thousand dollars Jones gets for his novel, and the five pounds Milton got for his epic. I have always thought Milton was paid too little, but I will own that he ought not to have been paid at all, if it comes to that. Again, I say that no man ought to live by any art; it is a shame to the art if not to the artist; but as yet there is no means of the artist's living otherwise, and continuing an artist.

The literary man has certainly no complaint to make of the newspaper man, generally speaking. I have often thought with amazement of the kindness shown by the press to our whole unworthy craft, and of the help so lavishly and freely given to rising and even risen authors. To put it coarsely, brutally, I do not suppose that any other business receives so much gratuitous advertising, except the theatre. It is enormous, the space given in the newspapers to literary notes, literary announcements, reviews, interviews, personal paragraphs, biographies, and all the rest, not to mention the vigorous and incisive attacks made from time to time upon different authors for their opinions of romanticism, realism, capitalism, socialism, Catholicism, and Sandemanianism. I have sometimes doubted whether the public cared for so much of it all as the editors gave them, but I have always said this under my breath, and I have thankfully taken my share of the common bounty. A curious fact, however, is that this vast newspaper publicity seems to have very little to do with an author's popularity, though ever so much with his notoriety. Those strange subterranean fellows who never come to the surface in the newspapers, except for a contemptuous paragraph at long intervals, outsell the famousest of the celebrities, and secretly have their horses and yachts and country seats, while immodest merit is left to get about on foot and look up summer board at the cheaper hotels. That is probably right, or it would not happen; it seems to be in the general scheme, like millionairism and pauperism; but it becomes a question, then, whether the newspapers, with all their friendship for literature, and their actual generosity to literary men, can really help one much to fortune, however much they help one to fame. Such a question is almost too dreadful, and though I have asked it, I will not attempt to answer it. I would much rather consider the question whether if the newspapers can make an author they can also unmake him, and I feel pretty safe in saying that I do not think they can. The Afreet once out of the bottle can never be coaxed back or cudgelled back; and the author whom the newspapers have made cannot be unmade by the newspapers. They consign him to oblivion with a rumor that fills the land, and they keep visiting him there with an uproar which attracts more and more notice to him. An author who has long enjoyed their favor, suddenly and rather mysteriously loses it, through his opinions on certain matters of literary taste, say. For the space of five or six years he is denounced with a unanimity and an incisive vigor that ought to convince him there is something wrong. If he thinks it is his censors, he clings to his opinions with an abiding constance, while ridicule, obloquy, caricature, burlesque, critical refutation and personal detraction follow unsparingly upon every expression, for instance, of his belief that romantic fiction is the highest form of fiction, and that the base, sordid, photographic, commonplace school of Tolstoy, Tourguenief, Zola, Hardy, and James, are unworthy a moment's comparison with the school of Rider Haggard. All this ought certainly to unmake the author in question, and strew his disjecta membra wide over the realm of oblivion. But this is not really the effect. Slowly but surely the clamor dies away, and the author, without relinquishing one of his wicked opinions, or in anywise showing himself repentant, remains apparently whole; and he even returns in a measure to the old kindness: not indeed to the earlier day of perfectly smooth things, but certainly to as much of it as he merits.

I would not have the young author, from this imaginary case, believe that it is well either to court or to defy the good opinion of the press. In fact, it will not only be better taste, but it will be better business for him to keep it altogether out of his mind. There is only one whom he can safely try to please, and that is himself. If he does this he will very probably please other people; but if he does not please himself he may be sure that he will not please them; the book which he has not enjoyed writing, no one will enjoy reading. Still, I would not have him attach too little consequence to the influence of the press. I should say, let him take the celebrity it gives him gratefully but not too seriously; let him reflect that he is often the necessity rather than the ideal of the paragrapher, and that the notoriety the journalists bestow upon him is not the measure of their acquaintance with his work, far less his meaning. They are good fellows, those poor, hard-pushed fellows of the press, but the very conditions of their censure, friendly or unfriendly, forbid it thoroughness, and it must often have more zeal than knowledge in it.

X.

Whether the newspapers will become the rivals of the magazines as the vehicle of literature is a matter that still remains in doubt with the careful observer, after a decade of the newspaper syndicate. Our daily papers never had the habit of the feuilleton as those of the European continent have it; they followed the English tradition in this, though they departed from it in so many other things; and it was not till the Sunday editions of the great dailies arose that there was any real hope for the serial in the papers. I suspect that it was the vast demand for material in their pages--twelve, eighteen, twenty-four, thirty-six--that created the syndicate, for it was the necessity of the Sunday edition not only to have material in abundance, but, with all possible regard for quality, to have it cheap; and the syndicate, when it came into being, imagined a means of meeting this want. It sold the same material to as many newspapers as it could for simultaneous publication in their Sunday editions, which had each its special field, and did not compete with another.

I do not think the syndicate began with serials, and I do not think it is likely to end with them. It has rather worked the vein of interviews, personal adventure, popular science, useful information, travel, sketches, and short stories. Still it has placed a good many serial stories, and at pretty good prices, but not generally so good as those the magazines pay the better sort of writers; for the worse sort it has offered perhaps the best market they have had out of book form. By the newspapers, the syndicate conceives, and perhaps justly, that something sensational is desired; yet all the serial stories it has placed cannot be called sensational. It has enlarged the field of belles-lettres, certainly, but not permanently, I think, in the case of the artistic novel. As yet the women, who form the largest, if not the only cultivated class among us, have not taken very cordially to the Sunday edition, except for its social gossip; they certainly do not go to it for their fiction, and its fiction is mainly of the inferior sort with which boys and men beguile their leisure.

In fact the newspapers prefer to remain newspapers, at least in quality if not in form; and I heard a story the other day from a charming young writer of his experience with them, which may have some instruction for the magazines that less wisely aim to become newspapers. He said that when he carried his work to the editors they struck out what he thought the best of it, because it was what they called magaziny; not contemptuously, but with an instinctive sense of what their readers wanted of them, and did not want. It was apparent that they did not want literary art, or even the appearance of it; they wanted their effects primary; they wanted their emotions raw, or at least saignantes from the joint of fact, and not prepared by the fancy or the taste.

The syndicate has no doubt advanced the prosperity of the short story by increasing the demand for it. We Americans had already done pretty well in that kind, for there was already a great demand for the short story in the magazines; but the syndicate of Sunday editions particularly cultivated it, and made it very paying.

I have heard that some short-story writers made the syndicate pay more for their wares than they got from the magazines for them, considering that the magazine publication could enhance their reputation, but the Sunday edition could do nothing for it. They may have been right or not in this; I will not undertake to say, but that was the business view of the case with them.

In spite of the fact that short stories when gathered into a volume and republished would not sell so well as a novel, the short story flourished, and its success in the periodicals began to be felt in the book trade: volumes of short stories suddenly began to sell. But now again, it is said the bottom has dropped out, and they do not sell, and their adversity in book form threatens to affect them in the magazines; an editor told me the other day that he had more short stories than he knew what to do with; and I was not offering him a short story of my own, either.

A permanent decline in the market for a kind of literary art which we have excelled in, or if we have not excelled, have done some of our most exquisite work, would be a pity.

There are other sorts of light literature once greatly in demand, but now apparently no longer desired by editors, who ought to know what their readers desire. Among these is the travel sketch, to me a very agreeable kind, and really to be regretted in its decline. There are some reasons for its decline besides a change of taste in readers, and a possible surfeit. Travel itself has become so universal that everybody, in a manner, has been everywhere, and the foreign scene has no longer the charm of strangeness. We do not think the Old World either so romantic or so ridiculous as we used; and perhaps from an instinctive perception of this altered mood writers no longer appeal to our sentiment or our humor with sketches of outlandish people and places. Of course this can hold true only in a general way; the thing is still done, but not nearly so much done as formerly. When one thinks of the long line of American writers who have greatly pleased in this sort, and who even got their first fame in it, one must grieve to see it obsolescent. Irving, Curtis, Bayard Taylor, Herman Melville, Ross Browne, Ik Marvell, Longfellow, Lowell, Story, Mr. James, Mr. Aldrich, Colonel Hay, Mr. Warner, Mrs. Hunt, Mr. C.W. Stoddard, Mark Twain, and many others whose names will not come to me at the moment, have in their several ways richly contributed to our pleasure in it; but I cannot now fancy a young author finding favor with an editor in a sketch of travel, or a study of foreign manners and customs; his work would have to be of the most signal importance and brilliancy to overcome the editor's feeling that the thing had been done already; and I believe that a publisher if offered a book of such things, would look at it askance, and plead the well-known quiet of the trade. Still, I may be mistaken.

I am rather more confident about the decline of another literary species, namely, the light essay. We have essays enough and to spare, of certain soberer and severer sorts, such as grapple with problems and deal with conditions; but the kind I mean, the slightly humorous, gentle, refined, and humane kind, seems no longer to abound as it once did. I do not know whether the editor discourages them, knowing his readers' frame, or whether they do not offer themselves, but I seldom find them in the magazines. I certainly do not believe that if anyone were now to write essays such as Mr. Warner's "Backlog Studies," an editor would refuse them; and perhaps nobody really writes them. Nobody seems to write the sort that Colonel Higginson formerly contributed to the periodicals, or such as Emerson wrote. Without a great name behind it, I am afraid that a volume of essays would find few buyers, even after the essays had made a public in the magazines. There are, of course, instances to the contrary, but they are not so many or so striking as to make me think that the essay could not be offered as a good opening for business talent.

I suspect that good poetry by well-known hands was never better paid in the magazines than it is now. I must say, too, that I think the quality of the minor poetry of our day is better than that of twenty-five or thirty years ago. I could name half a score of young poets whose work from time to time gives me great pleasure, by the reality of its feeling, and the delicate perfection of its art, but I will not name them, for fear of passing over half a score of others equally meritorious. We have certainly no reason to be discouraged, whatever reason the poets themselves have to be so, and I do not think that even in the short story our younger writers are doing better work than they are doing in the slighter forms of verse. Yet the notion of inviting business talent into this field would be as preposterous as that of asking it to devote itself to the essay. What book of verse by a recent poet, if we except some such peculiarly gifted poet as Mr. Whitcomb Riley, has paid its expenses, not to speak of any profit to the author? Of course, it would be rather more offensive and ridiculous that it should do so than that any other form of literary art should do so; and yet there is no more provision in our economic system for the support of the poet apart from his poems, than there is for the support of the novelist apart from his novel. One could not make any more money by writing poetry than by writing history, but it is a curious fact that while the historians have usually been rich men, and able to afford the luxury of writing history, the poets have usually been poor men, with no pecuniary justification in their devotion to a calling which is so seldom an election.

To be sure, it can be said for them that it costs far less to set up poet than to set up historian. There is no outlay for copying documents, or visiting libraries, or buying books. In fact, except as historian, the man of letters, in whatever walk, has not only none of the expenses of other men of business, but none of the expenses of other artists. He has no such outlay to make for materials, or models, or studio rent as the painter or the sculptor has, and his income, such as it is, is immediate. If he strikes the fancy of the editor with the first thing he offers, as he very well may, it is as well with him as with other men after long years of apprenticeship. Although he will always be the better for an apprenticeship, and the longer apprenticeship the better, he may practically need none at all. Such are the strange conditions of his acceptance with the public, that he may please better without it than with it. An author's first book is too often not only his luckiest, but really his best; it has a brightness that dies out under the school he puts himself to, but a painter or sculptor is only the gainer by all the school he can give himself.

XI.

In view of this fact it become again very hard to establish the author's status in the business world, and at moments I have grave question whether he belongs there at all, except as a novelist. There is, of course, no outlay for him in this sort, any more than in any other sort of literature, but it at least supposes and exacts some measure of preparation. A young writer may produce a brilliant and very perfect romance, just as he may produce a brilliant and very perfect poem, but in the field of realistic fiction, or in what we used to call the novel of manners, a writer can only produce an inferior book at the outset. For this work he needs experience and observation, not so much of others as of himself, for ultimately his characters will all come out of himself, and he will need to know motive and character with such thoroughness and accuracy as he can acquire only through his own heart. A man remains in a measure strange to himself as long as he lives, and the very sources of novelty in his work will be within himself; he can continue to give it freshness in no other way than by knowing himself better and better. But a young writer and an untrained writer has not yet begun to be acquainted even with the lives of other men. The world around him remains a secret as well as the world within him, and both unfold themselves simultaneously to that experience of joy and sorrow that can come only with the lapse of time. Until he is well on toward forty, he will hardly have assimilated the materials of a great novel, although he may have accumulated them. The novelist, then, is a man of letters who is like a man of business in the necessity of preparation for his calling, though he does not pay store-rent, and may carry all his affairs under his hat, as the phrase is. He alone among men of letters may look forward to that sort of continuous prosperity which follows from capacity and diligence in other vocations; for story-telling is now a fairly recognized trade, and the story-teller has a money-standing in the economic world. It is not a very high standing, I think, and I have expressed the belief that it does not bring him the respect felt for men in other lines of business. Still our people cannot deny some consideration to a man who gets a hundred dollars a thousand words. That is a fact appreciable to business, and the man of letters in the line of fiction may reasonably feel that his place in our civilization, though he may owe it to the women who form the great mass of his readers, has something of the character of a vested interest in the eyes of men. There is, indeed, as yet no conspiracy law which will avenge the attempt to injure him in his business. A critic, or a dark conjuration of critics, may damage him at will and to the extent of their power, and he has no recourse but to write better books, or worse. The law will do nothing for him, and a boycott of his books might be preached with immunity by any class of men not liking his opinions on the question of industrial slavery or antipaedobaptism. Still the market for his wares is steadier than the market for any other kind of literary wares, and the prices are better. The historian, who is a kind of inferior realist, has something like the same steadiness in the market, but the prices he can command are much lower, and the two branches of the novelist's trade are not to be compared in a business way. As for the essayist, the poet, the traveller, the popular scientist, they are nowhere in the competition for the favor of readers. The reviewer, indeed, has a pretty steady call for his work, but I fancy the reviewers who get a hundred dollars a thousand words could all stand upon the point of a needle without crowding one another; I should rather like to see them doing it. Another gratifying fact of the situation is that the best writers of fiction who are most in demand with the magazines, probably get nearly as much money for their work as the inferior novelists who outsell them by tens of thousands, and who make their appeal to the innumerable multitude of the less educated and less cultivated buyers of fiction in book-form. I think they earn their money, but if I did not think all of the higher class of novelists earned so much money as they get, I should not be so invidious as to single out for reproach those who did not.

The difficulty about payment, as I have hinted, is that literature has no objective value really, but only a subjective value, if I may so express it. A poem, an essay, a novel, even a paper on political economy, may be worth gold untold to one reader, and worth nothing whatever to another. It may be precious to one mood of the reader, and worthless to another mood of the same reader. How, then, is it to be priced, and how is it to be fairly marketed? All people must be fed, and all people must be clothed, and all people must be housed; and so meat, raiment, and shelter are things of positive and obvious necessity, which may fitly have a market price put upon them. But there is no such positive and obvious necessity, I am sorry to say, for fiction, or not for the higher sort of fiction. The sort of fiction which corresponds to the circus and the variety theatre in the show-business seems essential to the spiritual health of the masses, but the most cultivated of the classes can get on, from time to time, without an artistic novel. This is a great pity, and I should be very willing that readers might feel something like the pangs of hunger and cold, when deprived of their finer fiction; but apparently they never do. Their dumb and passive need is apt only to manifest itself negatively, or in the form of weariness of this author or that. The publisher of books can ascertain the fact through the declining sales of a writer; but the editor of a magazine, who is the best customer of the best writers, must feel the market with a much more delicate touch. Sometimes it may be years before he can satisfy himself that his readers are sick of Smith, and are pining for Jones; even then he cannot know how long their mood will last, and he is by no means safe in cutting down Smith's price and putting up Jones's. With the best will in the world to pay justly, he cannot. Smith, who has been boring his readers to death for a year, may write to-morrow a thing that will please them so much that he will at once be a prime favorite again; and Jones, whom they have been asking for, may do something so uncharacteristic and alien that it will be a flat failure in the magazine. The only thing that gives either writer positive value is his acceptance with the reader; but the acceptance is from month to month wholly uncertain. Authors are largely matters of fashion, like this style of bonnet, or that shape of gown. Last spring the dresses were all made with lace berthas, and Smith was read; this year the butterfly capes are worn, and Jones is the favorite author. Who shall forecast the fall and winter modes?

XII.

In this inquiry it is always the author rather than the publisher, always the contributor rather than the editor, whom I am concerned for. I study the difficulties of the publisher and editor only because they involve the author and the contributor; if they did not, I will not say with how hard a heart I should turn from them; my only pang now in scrutinizing the business conditions of literature is for the makers of literature, not the purveyors of it.

After all, and in spite of my vaunting title, is the man of letters ever a business man? I suppose that, strictly speaking, he never is, except in those rare instances where, through need or choice, he is the publisher as well as the author of his books. Then he puts something on the market and tries to sell it there, and is a man of business. But otherwise he is an artist merely, and is allied to the great mass of wage-workers who are paid for the labor they have put into the thing done or the thing made; who live by doing or making a thing, and not by marketing a thing after some other man has done it or made it. The quality of the thing has nothing to do with the economic nature of the case; the author is, in the last analysis, merely a workingman, and is under the rule that governs the workingman's life. If he is sick or sad, and cannot work, if he is lazy or tipsy and will not, then he earns nothing. He cannot delegate his business to a clerk or a manager; it will not go on while he is sleeping. The wage he can command depends strictly upon his skill and diligence.

I myself am neither sorry nor ashamed for this; I am glad and proud to be of those who eat their bread in the sweat of their own brows, and not the sweat of other men's brows; I think my bread is the sweeter for it. In the meantime I have no blame for business men; they are no more of the condition of things than we workingmen are; they did no more to cause it or create it; but I would rather be in my place than in theirs, and I wish that I could make all my fellow-artists realize that economically they are the same as mechanics, farmers, day-laborers. It ought to be our glory that we produce something, that we bring into the world something that was not choately there before; that at least we fashion or shape something anew; and we ought to feel the tie that binds us to all the toilers of the shop and field, not as a galling chain, but as a mystic bond also uniting us to Him who works hitherto and evermore.

I know very well that to the vast multitude of our fellow-workingmen we artists are the shadows of names, or not even the shadows. I like to look the facts in the face, for though their lineaments are often terrible, yet there is light nowhere else; and I will not pretend, in this light, that the masses care any more for us than we care for the masses, or so much. Nevertheless, and most distinctly, we are not of the classes. Except in our work, they have no use for us; if now and then they fancy qualifying their material splendor or their spiritual dulness with some artistic presence, the attempt is always a failure that bruises and abashes. In so far as the artist is a man of the world, he is the less an artist, and if he fashions himself upon fashion, he deforms his art. We all know that ghastly type; it is more absurd even than the figure which is really of the world, which was born and bred in it, and conceives of nothing outside of it, or above it. In the social world, as well as in the business world, the artist is anomalous, in the actual conditions, and he is perhaps a little ridiculous.

Yet he has to be somewhere, poor fellow, and I think that he will do well to regard himself as in a transition state. He is really of the masses, but they do not know it, and what is worse, they do not know him; as yet the common people do not hear him gladly or hear him at all. He is apparently of the classes; they know him, and they listen to him; he often amuses them very much; but he is not quite at ease among them; whether they know it or not, he knows that he is not of their kind. Perhaps he will never be at home anywhere in the world as long as there are masses whom he ought to consort with, and classes whom he cannot consort with. The prospect is not brilliant for any artist now living, but perhaps the artist of the future will see in the flesh the accomplishment of that human equality of which the instinct has been divinely planted in the human soul.

The Codes Of Hammurabi And Moses
W. W. Davies

QTY

The discovery of the Hammurabi Code is one of the greatest achievements of archaeology, and is of paramount interest, not only to the student of the Bible, but also to all those interested in ancient history...

Religion   ISBN: *1-59462-338-4*   **Pages:132**
MSRP $12.95

The Theory of Moral Sentiments
Adam Smith

QTY

This work from 1749. contains original theories of conscience amd moral judgment and it is the foundation for systemof morals.

Philosophy ISBN: *1-59462-777-0*   **Pages:536**
MSRP $19.95

Jessica's First Prayer
Hesba Stretton

QTY

In a screened and secluded corner of one of the many railway-bridges which span the streets of London there could be seen a few years ago, from five o'clock every morning until half past eight, a tidily set-out coffee-stall, consisting of a trestle and board, upon which stood two large tin cans, with a small fire of charcoal burning under each so as to keep the coffee boiling during the early hours of the morning when the work-people were thronging into the city on their way to their daily toil...

Pages:84

Childrens   ISBN: *1-59462-373-2*   *MSRP $9.95*

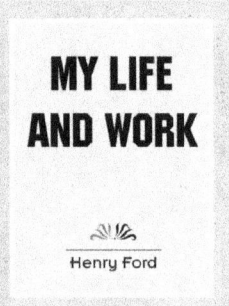

My Life and Work
Henry Ford

QTY

Henry Ford revolutionized the world with his implementation of mass production for the Model T automobile. Gain valuable business insight into his life and work with his own auto-biography... "We have only started on our development of our country we have not as yet, with all our talk of wonderful progress, done more than scratch the surface. The progress has been wonderful enough but..."

Pages:300

Biographies/   ISBN: *1-59462-198-5*   *MSRP $21.95*

The Art of Cross-Examination
Francis Wellman

QTY

I presume it is the experience of every author, after his first book is published upon an important subject, to be almost overwhelmed with a wealth of ideas and illustrations which could readily have been included in his book, and which to his own mind, at least, seem to make a second edition inevitable. Such certainly was the case with me; and when the first edition had reached its sixth impression in five months, I rejoiced to learn that it seemed to my publishers that the book had met with a sufficiently favorable reception to justify a second and considerably enlarged edition. ..

Pages:412

Reference   **ISBN:** *1-59462-647-2*   *MSRP $19.95*

On the Duty of Civil Disobedience
Henry David Thoreau

QTY

Thoreau wrote his famous essay, On the Duty of Civil Disobedience, as a protest against an unjust but popular war and the immoral but popular institution of slave-owning. He did more than write—he declined to pay his taxes, and was hauled off to gaol in consequence. Who can say how much this refusal of his hastened the end of the war and of slavery ?

Law   **ISBN:** *1-59462-747-9*   **Pages:48**

MSRP $7.45

Dream Psychology Psychoanalysis for Beginners
Sigmund Freud

QTY

Sigmund Freud, born Sigismund Schlomo Freud (May 6, 1856 - September 23, 1939), was a Jewish-Austrian neurologist and psychiatrist who co-founded the psychoanalytic school of psychology. Freud is best known for his theories of the unconscious mind, especially involving the mechanism of repression; his redefinition of sexual desire as mobile and directed towards a wide variety of objects; and his therapeutic techniques, especially his understanding of transference in the therapeutic relationship and the presumed value of dreams as sources of insight into unconscious desires.

Pages:196

Psychology   **ISBN:** *1-59462-905-6*   *MSRP $15.45*

The Miracle of Right Thought
Orison Swett Marden

QTY

Believe with all of your heart that you will do what you were made to do. When the mind has once formed the habit of holding cheerful, happy, prosperous pictures, it will not be easy to form the opposite habit. It does not matter how improbable or how far away this realization may see, or how dark the prospects may be, if we visualize them as best we can, as vividly as possible, hold tenaciously to them and vigorously struggle to attain them, they will gradually become actualized, realized in the life. But a desire, a longing without endeavor, a yearning abandoned or held indifferently will vanish without realization.

Pages:360

Self Help   **ISBN:** *1-59462-644-8*   *MSRP $25.45*

QTY

The Rosicrucian Cosmo-Conception Mystic Christianity by *Max Heindel* ISBN: *1-59462-188-8* **$38.95**
The Rosicrucian Cosmo-conception is not dogmatic, neither does it appeal to any other authority than the reason of the student. It is: not controversial, but is: sent forth in the, hope that it may help to clear... New Age/Religion Pages 646

Abandonment To Divine Providence by *Jean-Pierre de Caussade* ISBN: *1-59462-228-0* **$25.95**
"The Rev. Jean Pierre de Caussade was one of the most remarkable spiritual writers of the Society of Jesus in France in the 18th Century. His death took place at Toulouse in 1751. His works have gone through many editions and have been republished... Inspirational/Religion Pages 400

Mental Chemistry by *Charles Haanel* ISBN: *1-59462-192-6* **$23.95**
Mental Chemistry allows the change of material conditions by combining and appropriately utilizing the power of the mind. Much like applied chemistry creates something new and unique out of careful combinations of chemicals the mastery of mental chemistry... New Age Pages 354

The Letters of Robert Browning and Elizabeth Barret Barrett 1845-1846 vol II ISBN: *1-59462-193-4* **$35.95**
by *Robert Browning and Elizabeth Barrett* Biographies Pages 596

Gleanings In Genesis (volume I) by *Arthur W. Pink* ISBN: *1-59462-130-6* **$27.45**
Appropriately has Genesis been termed "the seed plot of the Bible" for in it we have, in germ form, almost all of the great doctrines which are afterwards fully developed in the books of Scripture which follow... Religion/Inspirational Pages 420

The Master Key by *L. W. de Laurence* ISBN: *1-59462-001-6* **$30.95**
In no branch of human knowledge has there been a more lively increase of the spirit of research during the past few years than in the study of Psychology, Concentration and Mental Discipline. The requests for authentic lessons in Thought Control, Mental Discipline and... New Age/Business Pages 422

The Lesser Key Of Solomon Goetia by *L. W. de Laurence* ISBN: *1-59462-092-X* **$9.95**
This translation of the first book of the "Lernegton" which is now for the first time made accessible to students of Talismanic Magic was done, after careful collation and edition, from numerous Ancient Manuscripts in Hebrew, Latin, and French... New Age/Occult Pages 92

Rubaiyat Of Omar Khayyam by *Edward Fitzgerald* ISBN: *1-59462-332-5* **$13.95**
Edward Fitzgerald, whom the world has already learned, in spite of his own efforts to remain within the shadow of anonymity, to look upon as one of the rarest poets of the century, was born at Bredfield, in Suffolk, on the 31st of March, 1809. He was the third son of John Purcell... Music Pages 172

Ancient Law by *Henry Maine* ISBN: *1-59462-128-4* **$29.95**
The chief object of the following pages is to indicate some of the earliest ideas of mankind, as they are reflected in Ancient Law, and to point out the relation of those ideas to modern thought. Religion/History Pages 452

Far-Away Stories by *William J. Locke* ISBN: *1-59462-129-2* **$19.45**
"Good wine needs no bush, but a collection of mixed vintages does. And this book is just such a collection. Some of the stories I do not want to remain buried for ever in the museum files of dead magazine-numbers an author's not unpardonable vanity..." Fiction Pages 272

Life of David Crockett by *David Crockett* ISBN: *1-59462-250-7* **$27.45**
"Colonel David Crockett was one of the most remarkable men of the times in which he lived. Born in humble life, but gifted with a strong will, an indomitable courage, and unremitting perseverance... Biographies/New Age Pages 424

Lip-Reading by *Edward Nitchie* ISBN: *1-59462-206-X* **$25.95**
Edward B. Nitchie, founder of the New York School for the Hard of Hearing, now the Nitchie School of Lip-Reading, Inc, wrote "LIP-READING Principles and Practice". The development and perfecting of this meritorious work on lip-reading was an undertaking... How-to Pages 400

A Handbook of Suggestive Therapeutics, Applied Hypnotism, Psychic Science ISBN: *1-59462-214-0* **$24.95**
by *Henry Munro* Health/New Age/Health/Self-help Pages 376

A Doll's House: and Two Other Plays by *Henrik Ibsen* ISBN: *1-59462-112-8* **$19.95**
Henrik Ibsen created this classic when in revolutionary 1848 Rome. Introducing some striking concepts in playwriting for the realist genre, this play has been studied the world over. Fiction/Classics/Plays 308

The Light of Asia by *sir Edwin Arnold* ISBN: *1-59462-204-3* **$13.95**
In this poetic masterpiece, Edwin Arnold describes the life and teachings of Buddha. The man who was to become known as Buddha to the world was born as Prince Gautama of India but he rejected the worldly riches and abandoned the reigns of power when... Religion/History/Biographies Pages 170

The Complete Works of Guy de Maupassant by *Guy de Maupassant* ISBN: *1-59462-157-8* **$16.95**
"For days and days, nights and nights, I had dreamed of that first kiss which was to consecrate our engagement, and I knew not on what spot I should put my lips..." Fiction/Classics Pages 240

The Art of Cross-Examination by *Francis L. Wellman* ISBN: *1-59462-309-0* **$26.95**
Written by a renowned trial lawyer, Wellman imparts his experience and uses case studies to explain how to use psychology to extract desired information through questioning. How-to/Science/Reference Pages 408

Answered or Unanswered? by *Louisa Vaughan* ISBN: *1-59462-248-5* **$10.95**
Miracles of Faith in China Religion Pages 112

The Edinburgh Lectures on Mental Science (1909) by *Thomas* ISBN: *1-59462-008-3* **$11.95**
This book contains the substance of a course of lectures recently given by the writer in the Queen Street Hall, Edinburgh. Its purpose is to indicate the Natural Principles governing the relation between Mental Action and Material Conditions... New Age/Psychology Pages 148

Ayesha by *H. Rider Haggard* ISBN: *1-59462-301-5* **$24.95**
Verily and indeed it is the unexpected that happens! Probably if there was one person upon the earth from whom the Editor of this, and of a certain previous history, did not expect to hear again... Classics Pages 380

Ayala's Angel by *Anthony Trollope* ISBN: *1-59462-352-X* **$29.95**
The two girls were both pretty, but Lucy who was twenty-one who supposed to be simple and comparatively unattractive, whereas Ayala was credited, as her Bombwhat romantic name might show, with poetic charm and a taste for romance. Ayala when her father died was nineteen... Fiction Pages 484

The American Commonwealth by *James Bryce* ISBN: *1-59462-286-8* **$34.45**
An interpretation of American democratic political theory. It examines political mechanics and society from the perspective of Scotsman James Bryce Politics Pages 572

Stories of the Pilgrims by *Margaret P. Pumphrey* ISBN: *1-59462-116-0* **$17.95**
This book explores pilgrims religious oppression in England as well as their escape to Holland and eventual crossing to America on the Mayflower, and their early days in New England... History Pages 268

www.bookjungle.com *email: sales@bookjungle.com fax: 630-214-0564 mail: Book Jungle PO Box 2226 Champaign, IL 61825*

QTY

The Fasting Cure *by Sinclair Upton*   ISBN: *1-59462-222-1* **$13.95**
In the Cosmopolitan Magazine for May, 1910, and in the Contemporary Review (London) for April, 1910, I published an article dealing with my experiences in fasting. I have written a great many magazine articles, but never one which attracted so much attention... New Age/Self Help/Health Pages 164

Hebrew Astrology *by Sepharial*   ISBN: *1-59462-308-2* **$13.45**
In these days of advanced thinking it is a matter of common observation that we have left many of the old landmarks behind and that we are now pressing forward to greater heights and to a wider horizon than that which represented the mind-content of our progenitors... Astrology Pages 144

Thought Vibration or The Law of Attraction in the Thought World   ISBN: *1-59462-127-6* **$12.95**
by William Walker Atkinson   Psychology/Religion Pages 144

Optimism *by Helen Keller*   ISBN: *1-59462-108-X* **$15.95**
Helen Keller was blind, deaf, and mute since 19 months old, yet famously learned how to overcome these handicaps, communicate with the world, and spread her lectures promoting optimism. An inspiring read for everyone... Biographies/Inspirational Pages 84

Sara Crewe *by Frances Burnett*   ISBN: *1-59462-360-0* **$9.45**
In the first place, Miss Minchin lived in London. Her home was a large, dull, tall one, in a large, dull square, where all the houses were alike, and all the sparrows were alike, and where all the door-knockers made the same heavy sound... Childrens/Classic Pages 88

The Autobiography of Benjamin Franklin *by Benjamin Franklin*   ISBN: *1-59462-135-7* **$24.95**
The Autobiography of Benjamin Franklin has probably been more extensively read than any other American historical work, and no other book of its kind has had such ups and downs of fortune. Franklin lived for many years in England, where he was agent... Biographies/History Pages 332

Name	
Email	
Telephone	
Address	
City, State ZIP	

☐ **Credit Card**   ☐ **Check / Money Order**

Credit Card Number	
Expiration Date	
Signature	

Please Mail to: Book Jungle
PO Box 2226
Champaign, IL 61825
or Fax to: 630-214-0564

ORDERING INFORMATION

web*: www.bookjungle.com*
email*: sales@bookjungle.com*
fax*: 630-214-0564*
mail*: Book Jungle PO Box 2226 Champaign, IL 61825*
or PayPal *to sales@bookjungle.com*

Please contact us for bulk discounts

DIRECT-ORDER TERMS

**20% Discount if You Order
Two or More Books**
Free Domestic Shipping!
Accepted: Master Card, Visa,
Discover, American Express